Baseballasaurus

Written by Shirin Rahman

Illustrated by Dr. Gina Rizzo

Anky's smile was wide, and warm as sunshine. He loved baseball season!

"I'm going to be a Baseballasaurus," he said.

"Uh oh," said Eddie. "Anky, watch that tail."

"Ready, Anky?" Coach said.

Anky's happiness bubbled over as he marched onto the pitching mound.

"I can do this," Anky said, standing tall.

He stopped midway . . . and stared in wonder at the clouds floating across the sky.

His heart fluttered in delight. A butterfly!

Coach yelled. "Anky, can you PLEASE pay attention?"

Anky's head
drooped.

Eddie batted beautifully.

Stella pitched perfectly..

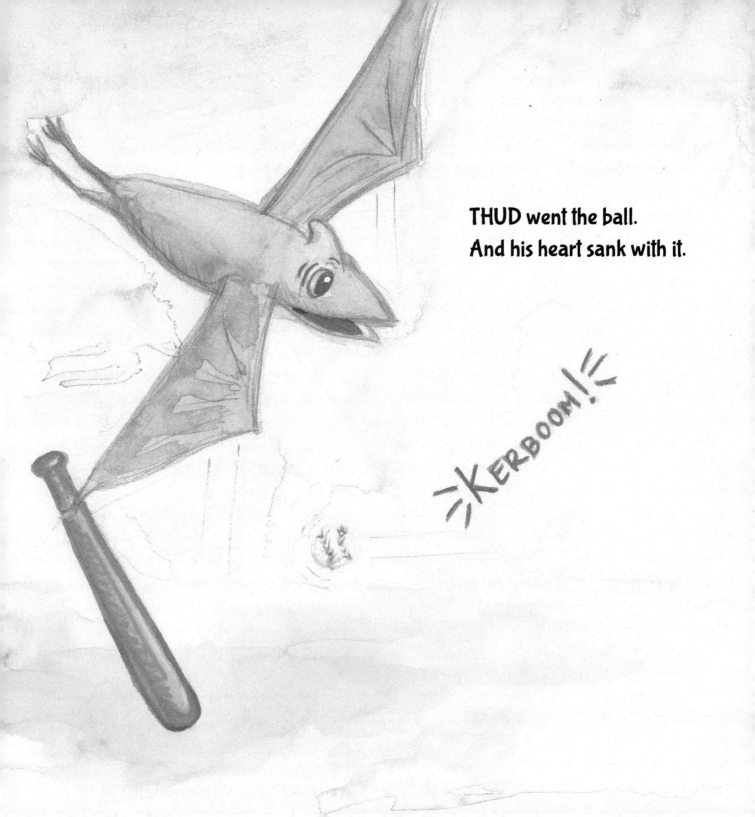

THUD went the ball.
And his heart sank with it.

On the outfield . . . he was distracted by the sun dancing across the lush green grass.

And missed the ball every time.

Coach made him last batter.

And Anky struck out every time.

He whispered.
"I wish I could do better."

Anky walked away, his head sunk low. "I need to practice,"

He practiced, but the bat didn't quite fit in his grasp.

"Will I ever be a Baseballasaurus?"
Anky wondered in the starry stillness.

Anky listened to the quiet of the night.
He took deep breaths into his belly.
"The sun does what the sun must do. The moon
does what the moon must do," he said to himself.

"Eddie and Stella are awesome players.
But I'm not Eddie. I'm not Stella.
I'm Anky and I'm good enough," he decided.
"I will shine in my own way," he said.

The next day, Anky walked onto the field with his head held high. Today, is a super awesome day!"
Hope bounced in his heart like fizzy bubbles.

"Good attitude, Anky," said Coach. "You have great team spirit."

At the game, someone yelled,
"Oh no! Not Anky!"

Anky's heart felt heavier than his armor plates.
He lumbered off the field, where no one saw his tears.

"Where's Anky," called Coach. "It is his turn at bat."

Anky took five deep belly breaths and walked across the field, ready to play.

The crowd watched.
"I can do it," Anky breathed and focused. "I can!"

Anky was ready.to play. But the bat was broken.

"I will play my way. I can do it," he said. "I can."

Anky turned,
he spun around . . .

Everyone ducked . . .

Anky swung his **TAIL**

WHACK!

UP.

UP,

The ball went **UP,**

The crowd gasped.

"Home run!" they cheered.

"Great job, Anky," said Coach.

"YAY! You did it!" Eddie and Stella yelled.

Anky smiled. "I knew I could."

"I'm a Baseballasaurus!"

AUTHOR'S NOTE

Ankylosauruses lived 68-66 million years ago during the late Cretaceous period. The name Ankylosaurus means 'fused lizard' because, like a tank, it was covered with bony plates.

Ankylosaurus's club tail was used for defending itself against predators like Tyrannosaurus Rex.

They ate a diet of leaves, ferns and soft vegetation and were slow-moving and sluggish. At between 4-8 tons, an Ankylosaurus was no lightweight.

Ankylosauruses lived at the same time as the Edmontosaurus and Struthiomimus. Unlike Edmontosaurus and Struthiomimus, the Ankylosaurus was a quadruped, meaning it walked on all fours. Their fossils have been found on the western plains of North America. The Museum of the Rockies in Montana is known to house the largest paleontological collection in the USA.

Baseballasaurus
Copyright © 2022 By Shirin Rahman
Artwork Copyright © 2022 By Dr. Gina Rizzo

Summary: Anky marches to the beat of his own drum - and sometimes that is tough. Will Anky ever be good at baseball? Will he ever be like his friends, Eddie and Stella?

Clear Fork Publishing
P.O. Box 870
102 S. Swenson
Stamford, Texas 79553
(325)773-5550
www.clearforkpublishing.com

Printed and Bound in the United States of America.

ISBN - 978-1-950169-57-3

Dedication:

For my precious children, Shaheed, Sabeen, Nadia, may you continue to shine your beautiful light. - S. R.

My illustrations are dedicated to my brothers and sisters and nieces and nephews. They have brought much joy to the world by always being themselves. Also, my artwork is dedicated to those of us who have felt we were not good enough. Anky shows us that by being ourselves and using our unique abilities we win which is better than "fitting in". - G. R.

Shirin Rahman
Author

Shirin is the author of several children's books. She and her husband have raised their three children in the suburbs of Chicago, Illinois. Now an empty nester, Shirin spends her days creating stories for children, in the hope that her words will inspire more empathy and understanding, compassion and kindness in the world.

www.ShirinShamsi.com

Gina Rizzo
Illustrator

Born to artists in Los Angeles, Gina has been an artist for her entire life. Where some children were given sporting equipment her toys were colored soaps to cover the walls of their bathroom with murals. After receiving a Bachelor of Arts in art with a minor in humanities from San Francisco State University, she earned two teaching credentials and a Master of Arts in Teaching from Chapman University and taught art at the high school level for ten years. After teaching nearly all grade levels for seventeen years, Gina became a PhD candidate at the California Institute of Integral Studies in San Francisco researching why the arts exist and is starting a diversity gift business selling educational and whimsical images on gift items that depict the range of human diversity DrGinaRizzo.com.

CPSIA information can be obtained
at www.ICGtesting.com
Printed in the USA
BVHW021044120422
634070BV00004B/432